CIRCUS · · · · · · · PARADE

BY **Harriet Ziefert**

PICTURES BY **Tanya Roitman**

BLUE APPLE BOOKS

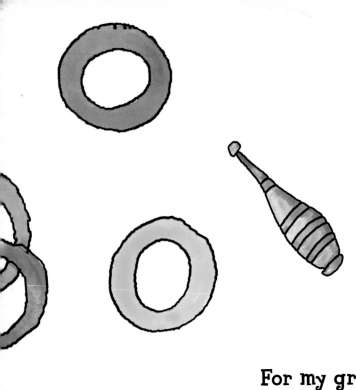

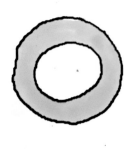

To my children,
Ilya, Greg, and Masha
—T. R.

For my granddaughter,
Sylvie Anne
—H. Z.

Text copyright © 2005 by Harriet Ziefert
Pictures copyright © 2005 by Tanya Roitman
All rights reserved
CIP Data is available.
Published in the United States 2005 by
Blue Apple Books
515 Valley Street, Maplewood, N.J. 07040
www.blueapplebooks.com
Distributed in the U.S. by Chronicle Books

First Edition
Printed in China
ISBN: 1-59354-088-4
1 3 5 7 9 10 8 6 4 2

A parade! A parade!
A circus parade!

A rat-a-tat-tat, a rum-a-tee-tum . . .
Sounds the beat of the first snare drum.

A dancing dog from Kalamazoo
Shows the crowd what he can do.

Flags are waving! Horns are blowing!
Hear the cheers. The crowd is growing.

Horns and drums and marching feet.
Feel that rhythm? Catch the beat!

Now here comes a big bass drum.

A-rum-a-tee-tum! A-rum-a-tee-tum!

A clown is pedaling down the street.

We know him by his nose and feet.

An elephant's walking down the street.

We know him by his trunk and feet.

Next come the horses, snorting, prancing.

On one of them a girl is dancing.

A band of clowns drives down the street.

Feel the rhythm. Catch the beat!

Majorettes in marching hats . . .

Strong man, jugglers, acrobats . . .

Man up high and dog down low . . .

Riding, walking, there they go!

Rum-a-tee tum—and still they come!
A-rum-a-tee . . . rum-a-tee . . . rum-a-tee tum!

A bear, a seal, a girl on a ball—
but that's not all!

One last band rolls down the street
With a big bass drum to keep the beat—

And still one little drum to come—
A-rum-a-tee tum, a-rum-a-tee tum...

A-rum-a-tee ... rum-a-tee ...

rum-a-tee-tum!

Bears in cars, clowns on bikes,

Girls on horses, clowns on trikes,

Monkeys, drummers, and dogs in hats,

Strong men, jugglers, acrobats.

Big brass bands to keep the beat

As they all march down the street.

Music and feet. Music and feet.

Feel the rhythm. Catch the beat!